STAR WARS®
INFINITIES
THE EMPIRE STRIKES BACK™

VOLUME FOUR

Script
DAVE LAND

Pencils
DAVIDÉ FABBRI

Inks
CHRISTIAN DALLA VECCHIA

Colors
DAN JACKSON

Lettering
STEVE DUTRO

Cover Art
CHRIS BACHALO WITH TIM TOWNSEND

In the aftermath of Luke Skywalker's death on the icy world of Hoth, Princess Leia has begun Jedi training with the ancient Jedi Master Yoda, who has revealed to Leia her relationship with both Luke and the evil Darth Vader.

Meanwhile, Han Solo, Chewbacca, and R2-D2—after a bungled attempt to repay Jabba the Hutt and clear Han's name—have managed to escape from Jabba's palace. Unfortunately, C-3PO was left behind in the confusion and has fallen into the hands of Darth Vader.

From the information in C-3PO's memory circuits, Vader was able to learn that Yoda is alive and living on Dagobah—and training a new Jedi . . . the offspring of Anakin Skywalker!

THE *STAR WARS INFINITIES* SERIES ASKS THE QUESTION: WHAT IF ONE THING HAPPENED DIFFERENTLY FROM WHAT WE SAW IN THE CLASSIC FILMS?

Spotlight

DARK HORSE COMICS

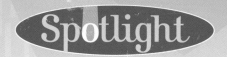

Visit us at www.abdopublishing.com

Reinforced library bound edition published in 2011 by Spotlight, a division of the ABDO Group, 8000 West 78th Street, Edina, Minnesota 55439. Spotlight produces high-quality reinforced library bound editions for schools and libraries. Published by agreement with Dark Horse Comics, Inc., and Lucasfilm Ltd.

Printed in the United States of America, North Mankato, Minnesota.
102010
012011
♻ This book contains at least 10% recycled materials.

Library of Congress Cataloging-in-Publication Data

Land, David.
   The empire strikes back / script, Dave Land ; art, Davidé Fabbri. -- Reinforced library bound ed.
      v. cm. -- (Star wars. Infinities)
   ISBN 978-1-59961-849-4 (vol. 1) -- ISBN 978-1-59961-850-0 (vol. 2) -- ISBN 978-1-59961-851-7 (vol. 3) -- ISBN 978-1-59961-852-4 (vol. 4)
   1. Graphic novels. [1. Graphic novels. 2. Science fiction.] I. Fabbri, Davide, ill. II. Title.
   PZ7.7.L35Emp 2011
   741.5'973--dc22
                              2010020248

All Spotlight books have reinforced library bindings and are manufactured in the United States of America.

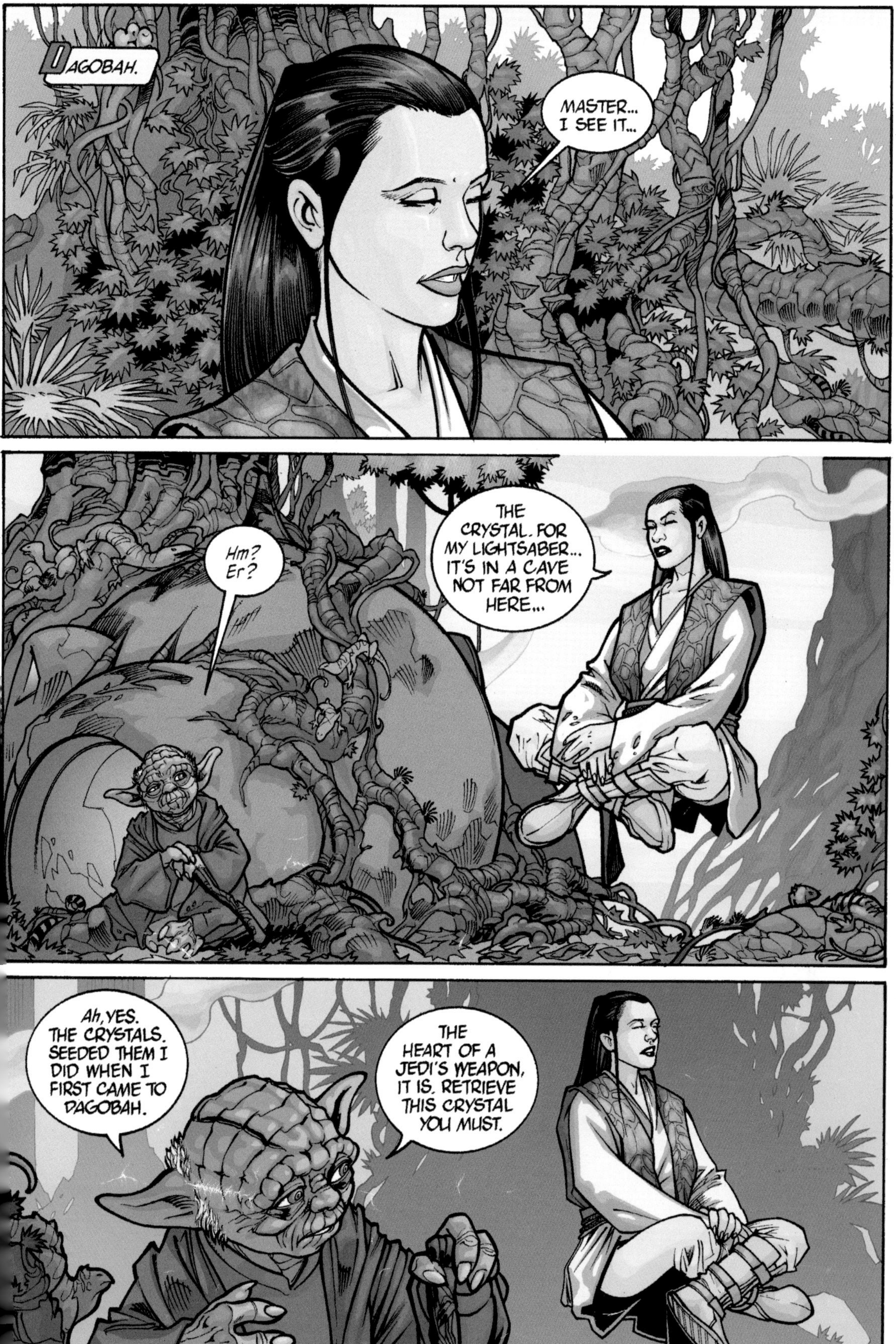
DAGOBAH.
MASTER... I SEE IT...
Hm? Er?
THE CRYSTAL. FOR MY LIGHTSABER... IT'S IN A CAVE NOT FAR FROM HERE...
Ah, YES. THE CRYSTALS. SEEDED THEM I DID WHEN I FIRST CAME TO DAGOBAH.
THE HEART OF A JEDI'S WEAPON, IT IS. RETRIEVE THIS CRYSTAL YOU MUST.

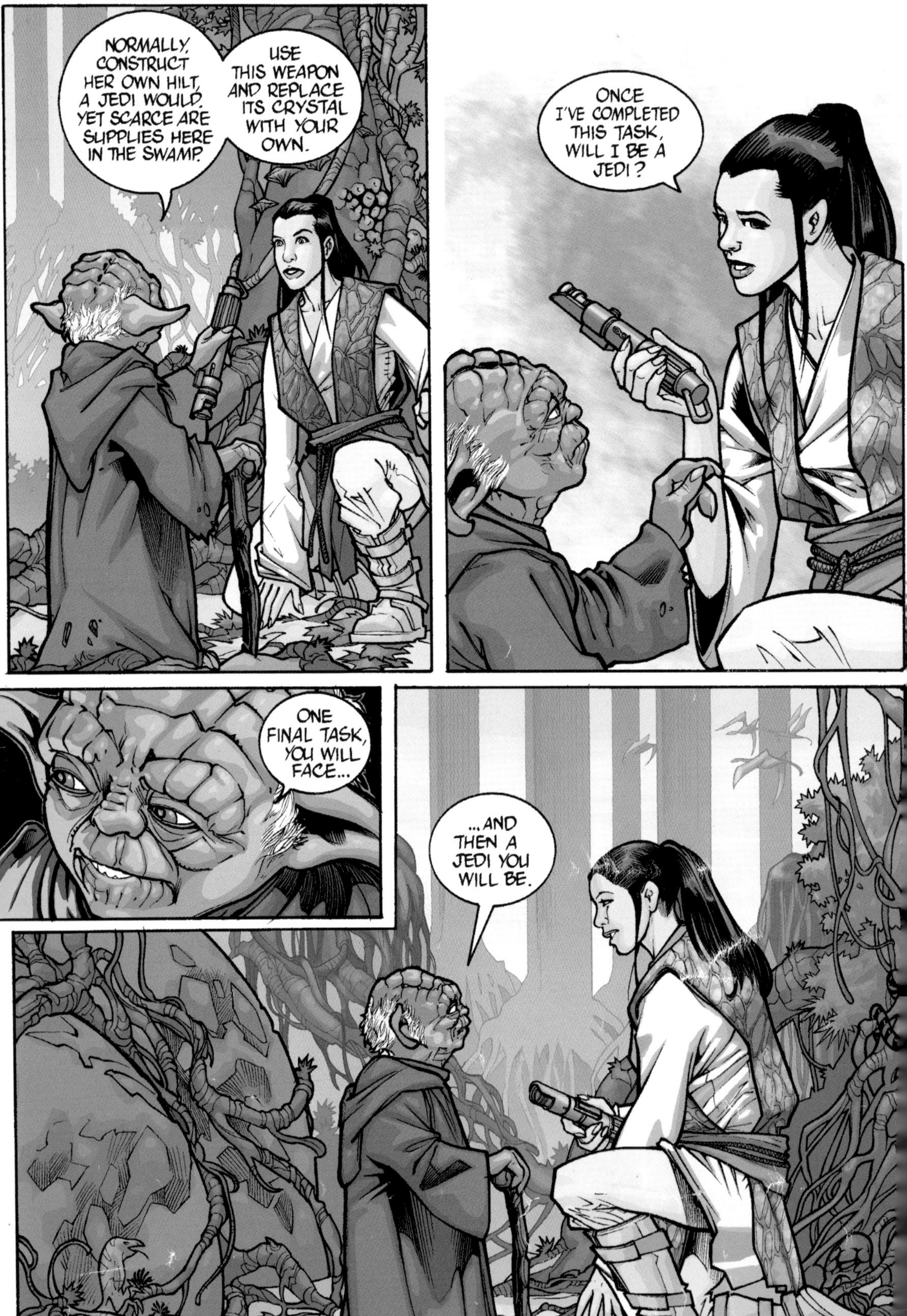
NORMALLY, CONSTRUCT HER OWN HILT, A JEDI WOULD. YET SCARCE ARE SUPPLIES HERE IN THE SWAMP.
USE THIS WEAPON AND REPLACE ITS CRYSTAL WITH YOUR OWN.
ONCE I'VE COMPLETED THIS TASK, WILL I BE A JEDI?
ONE FINAL TASK, YOU WILL FACE...
...AND THEN A JEDI YOU WILL BE.

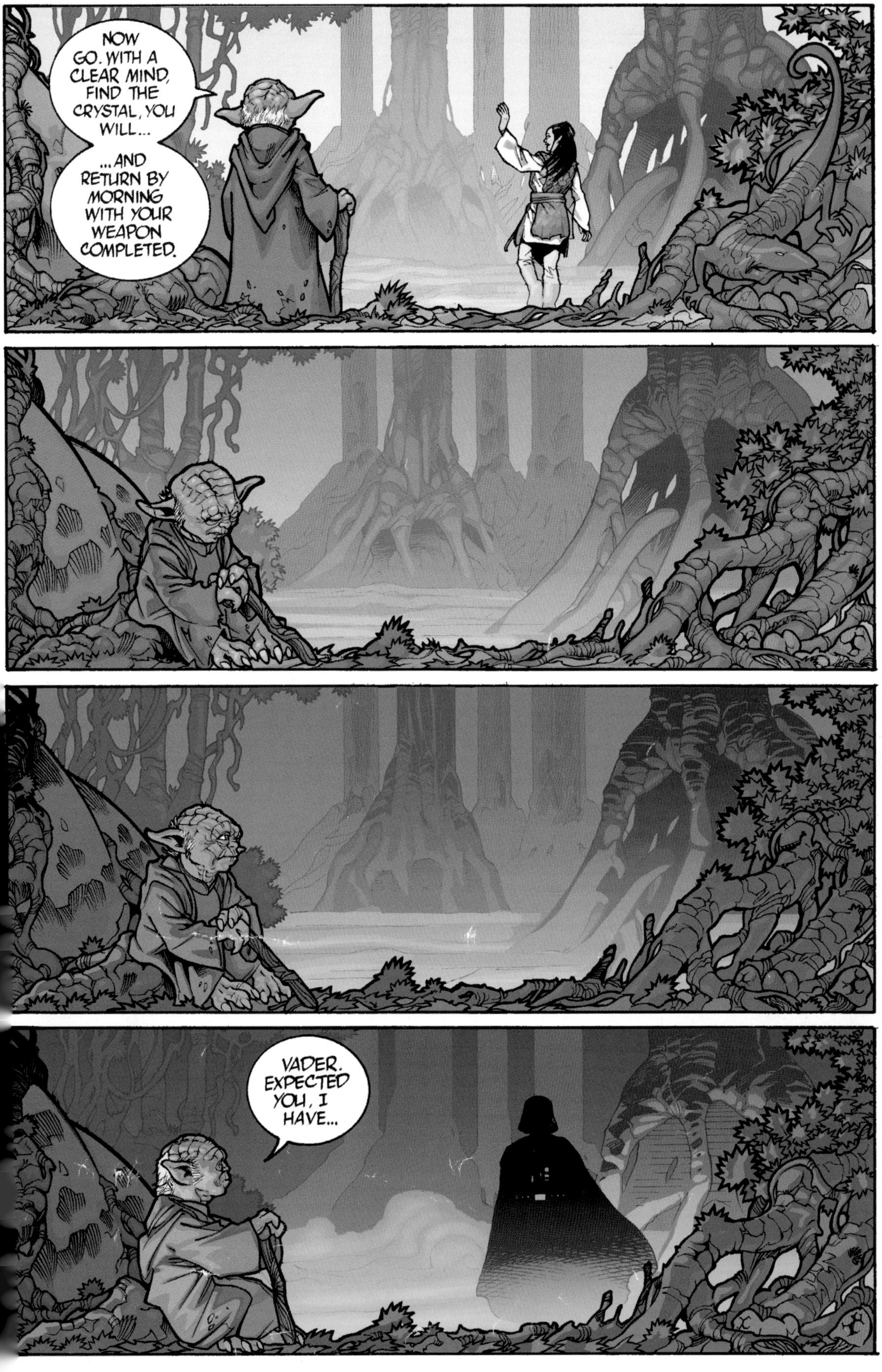
NOW GO. WITH A CLEAR MIND, FIND THE CRYSTAL, YOU WILL...
...AND RETURN BY MORNING WITH YOUR WEAPON COMPLETED.
VADER. EXPECTED YOU, I HAVE...

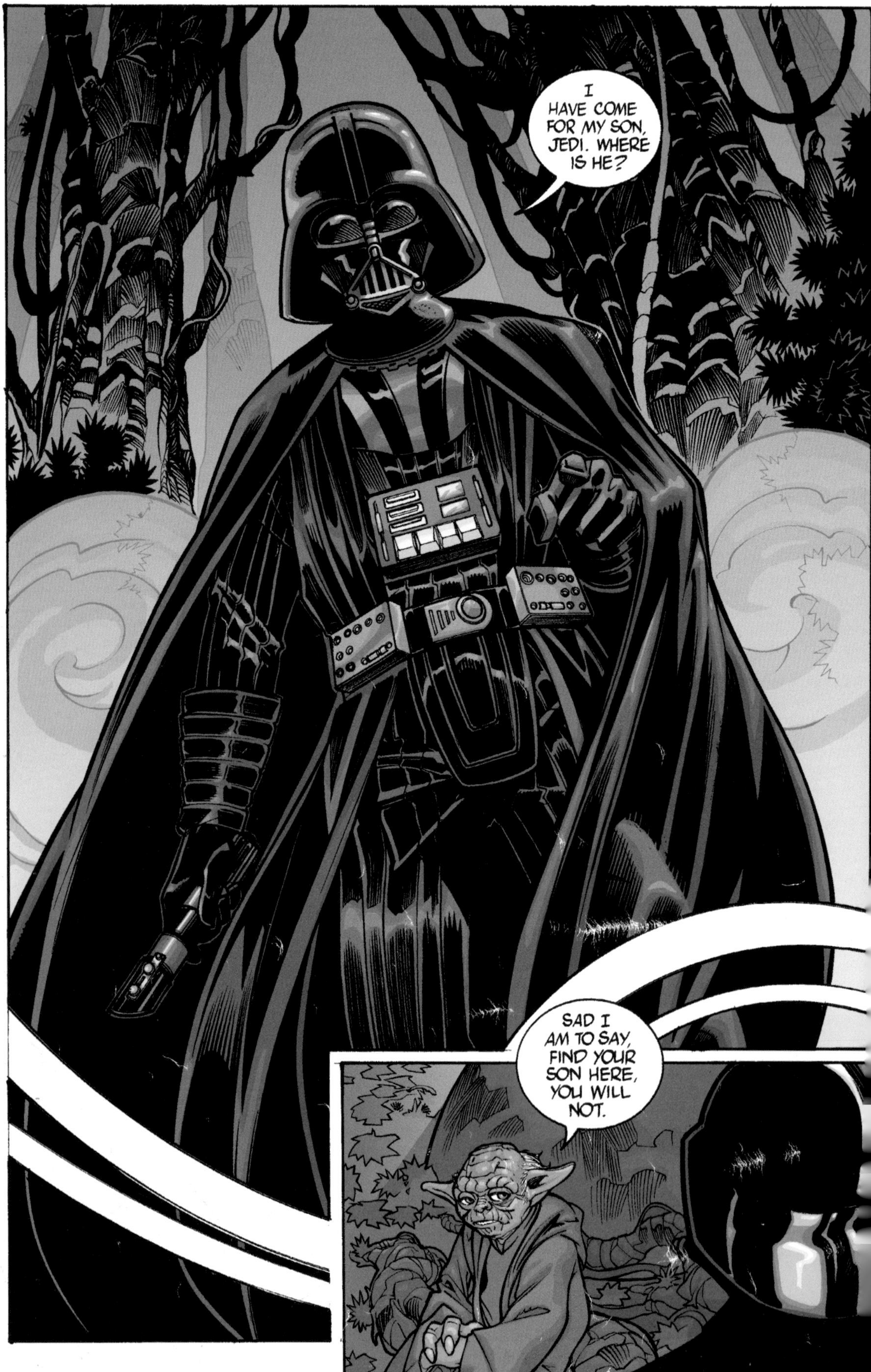
I HAVE COME FOR MY SON, JEDI. WHERE IS HE?
SAD I AM TO SAY, FIND YOUR SON HERE, YOU WILL NOT.

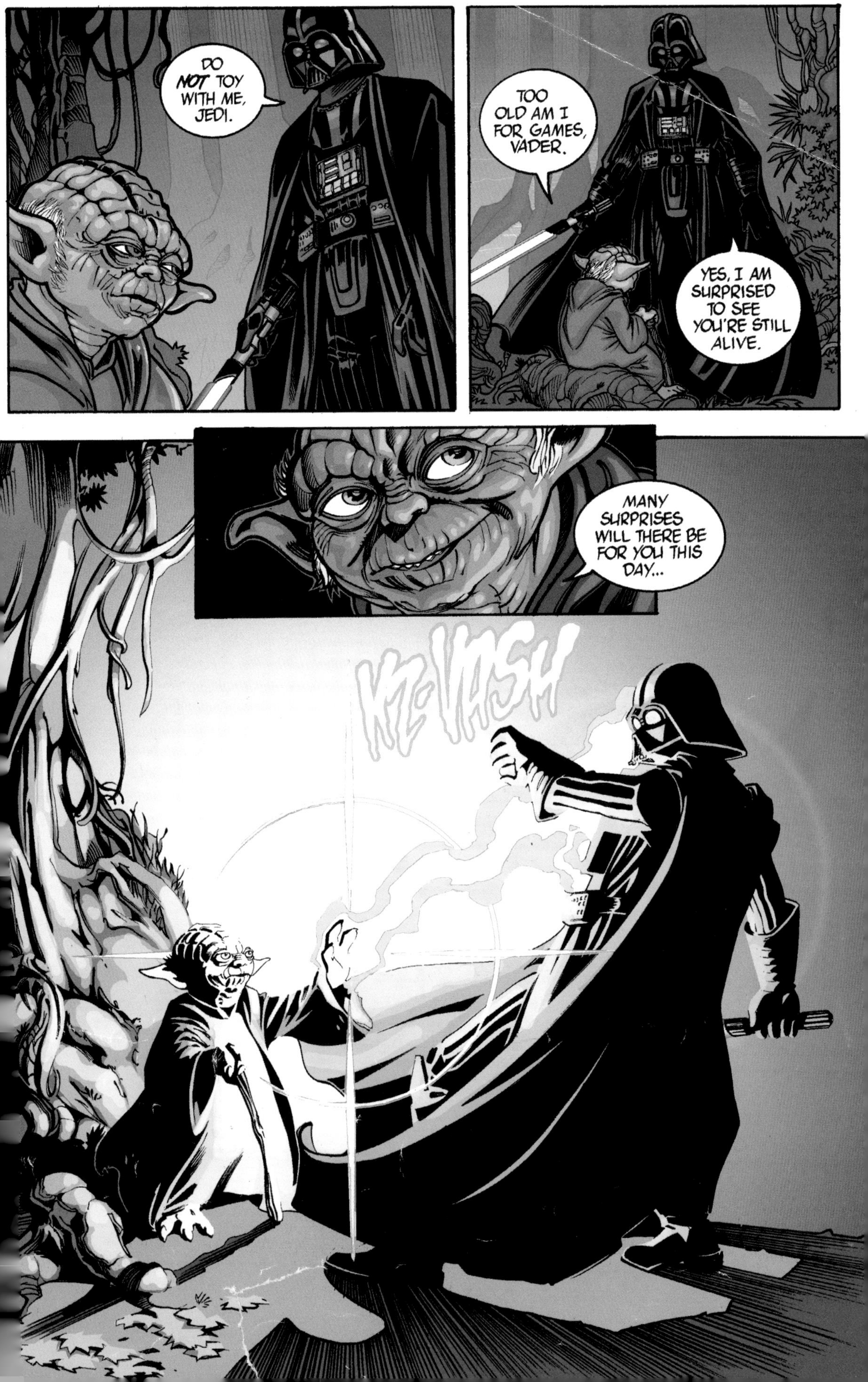
DO NOT TOY WITH ME, JEDI.
TOO OLD AM I FOR GAMES, VADER.
YES, I AM SURPRISED TO SEE YOU'RE STILL ALIVE.
MANY SURPRISES WILL THERE BE FOR YOU THIS DAY...
KZ-VASH

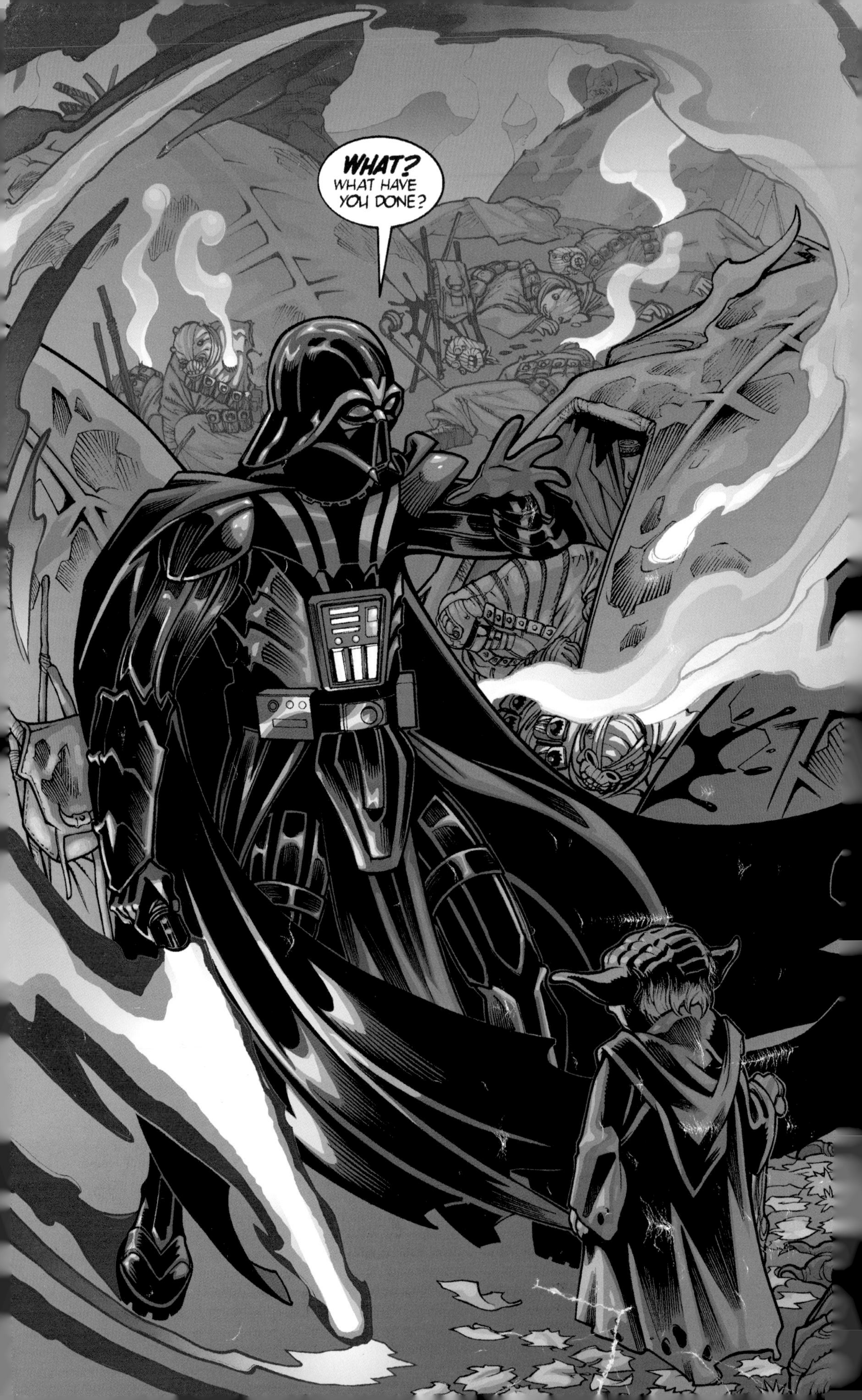
WHAT? WHAT HAVE YOU DONE?

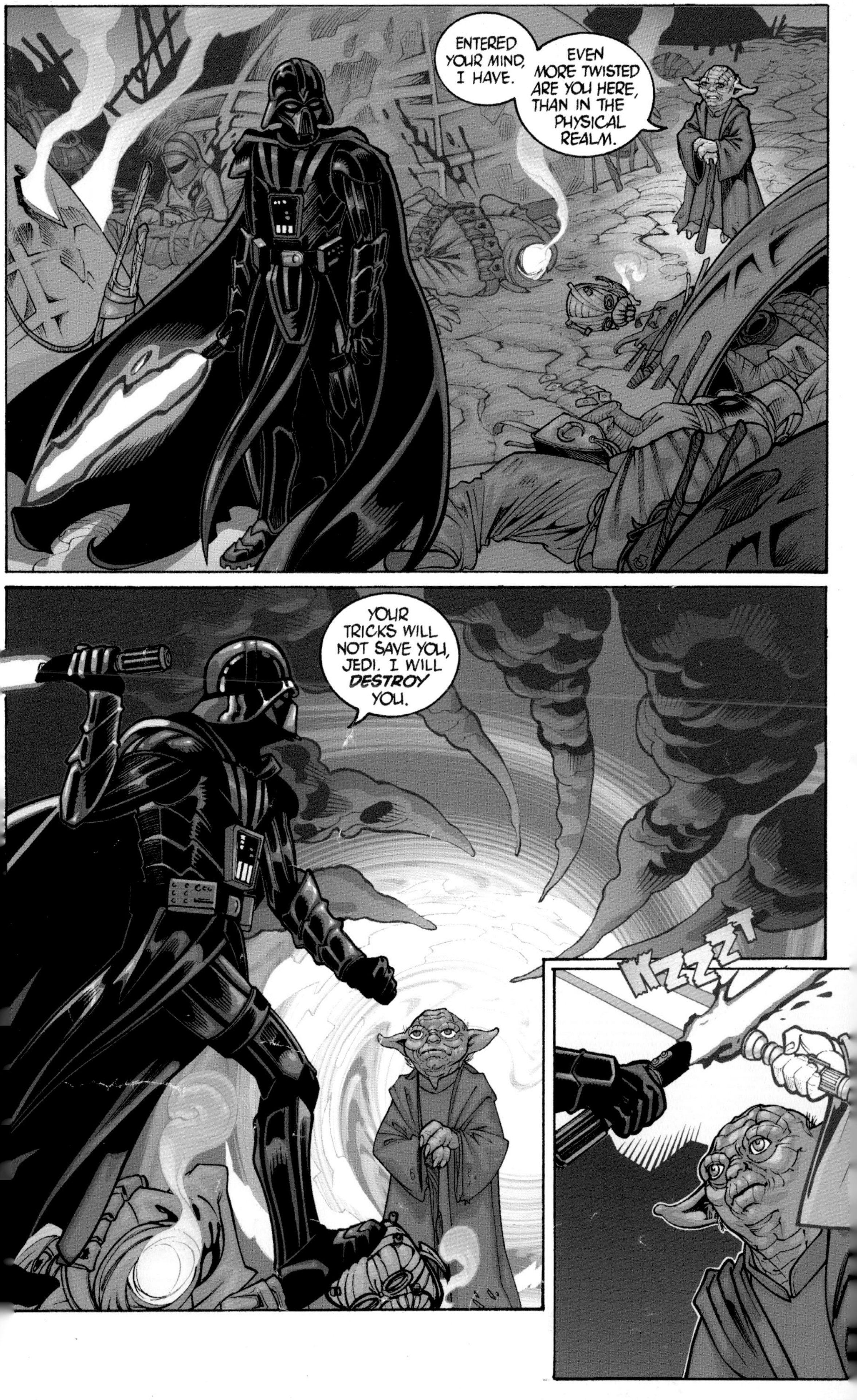
ENTERED YOUR MIND, I HAVE.
EVEN MORE TWISTED ARE YOU HERE, THAN IN THE PHYSICAL REALM.
YOUR TRICKS WILL NOT SAVE YOU, JEDI. I WILL DESTROY YOU.
KZZZT

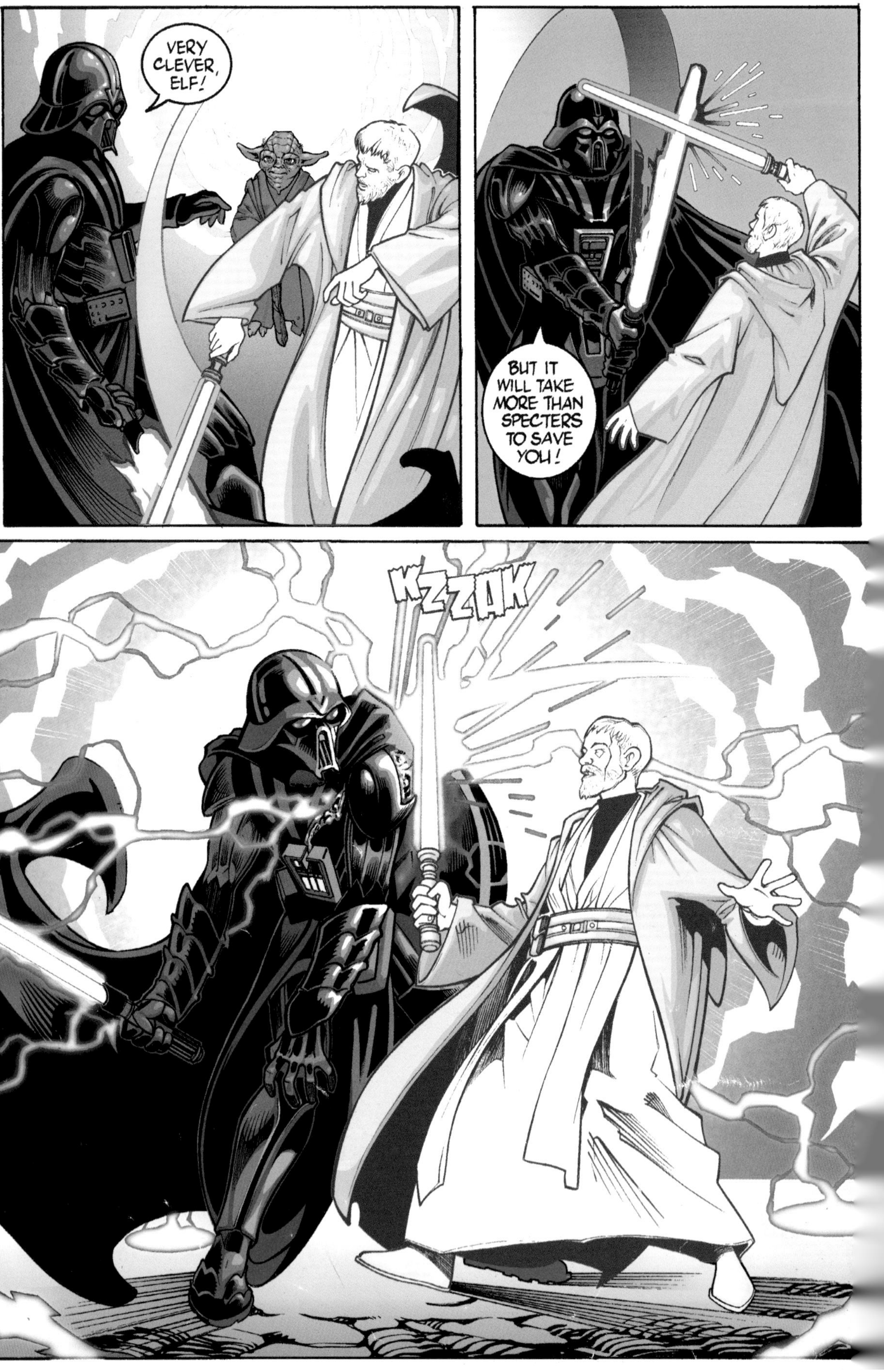
VERY CLEVER, ELF!
BUT IT WILL TAKE MORE THAN SPECTERS TO SAVE YOU!
KZZAK

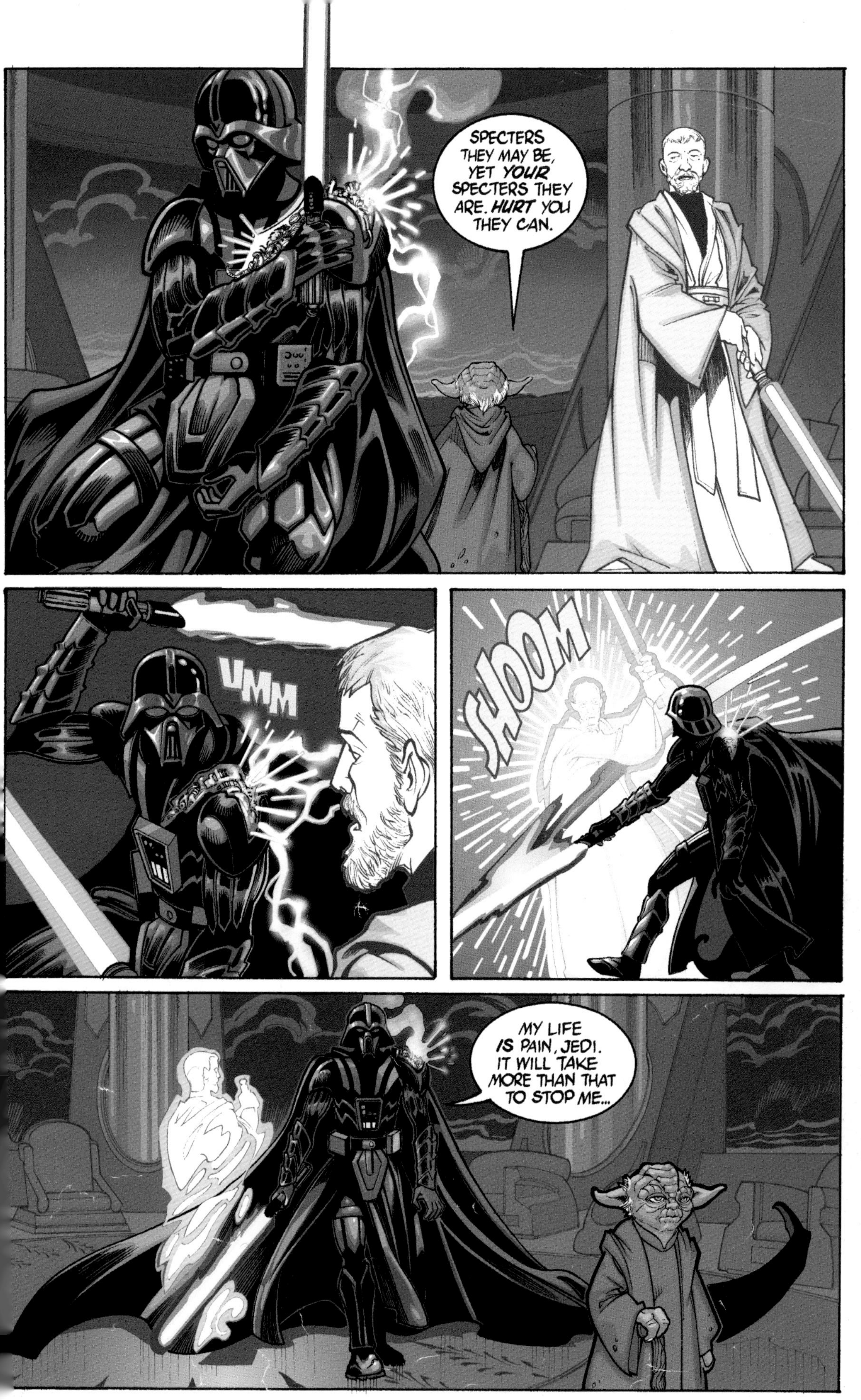
SPECTERS THEY MAY BE, YET YOUR SPECTERS THEY ARE. HURT YOU THEY CAN.
UMM
SHOOM
MY LIFE IS PAIN, JEDI. IT WILL TAKE MORE THAN THAT TO STOP ME...

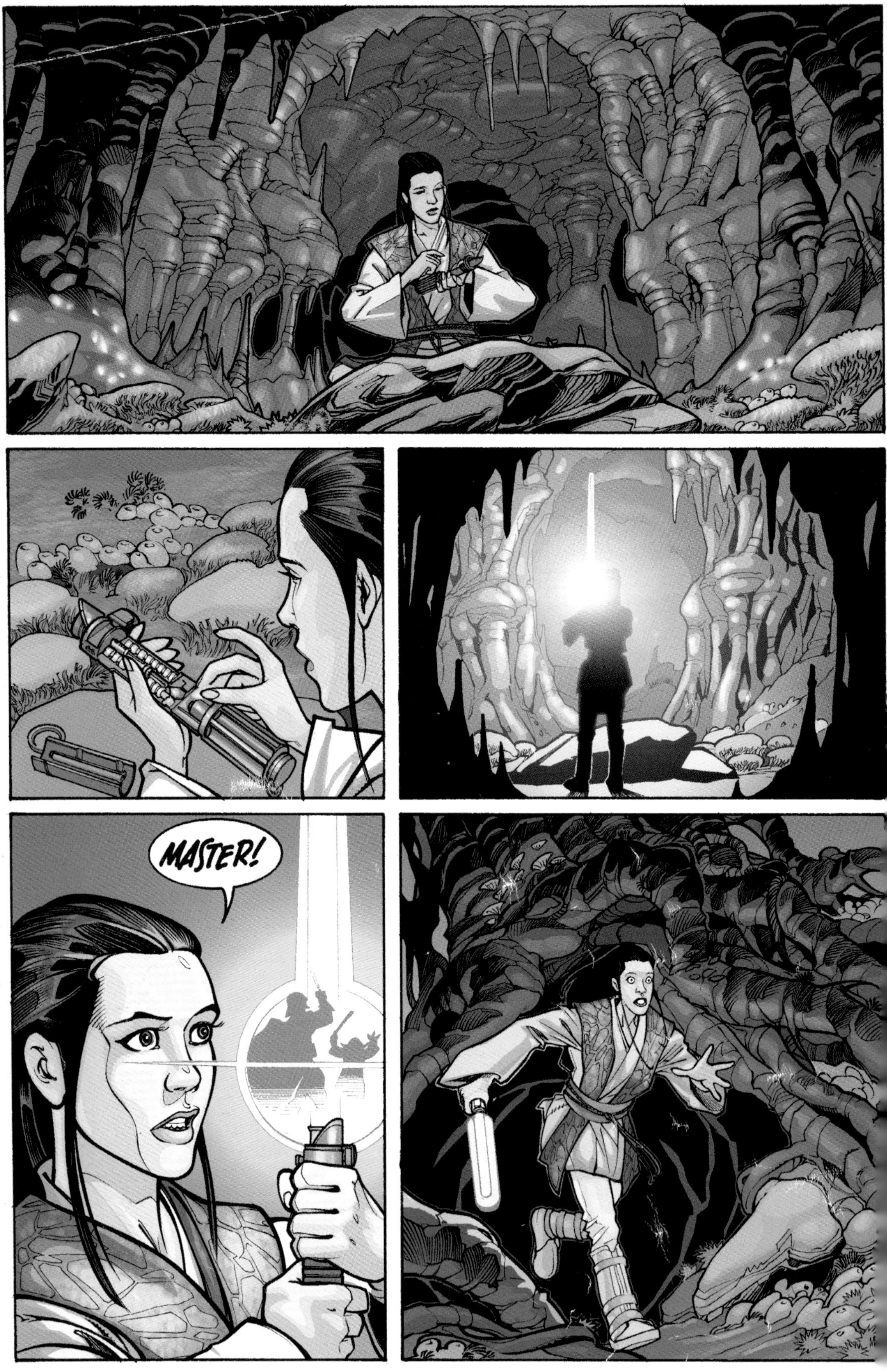
MASTER!

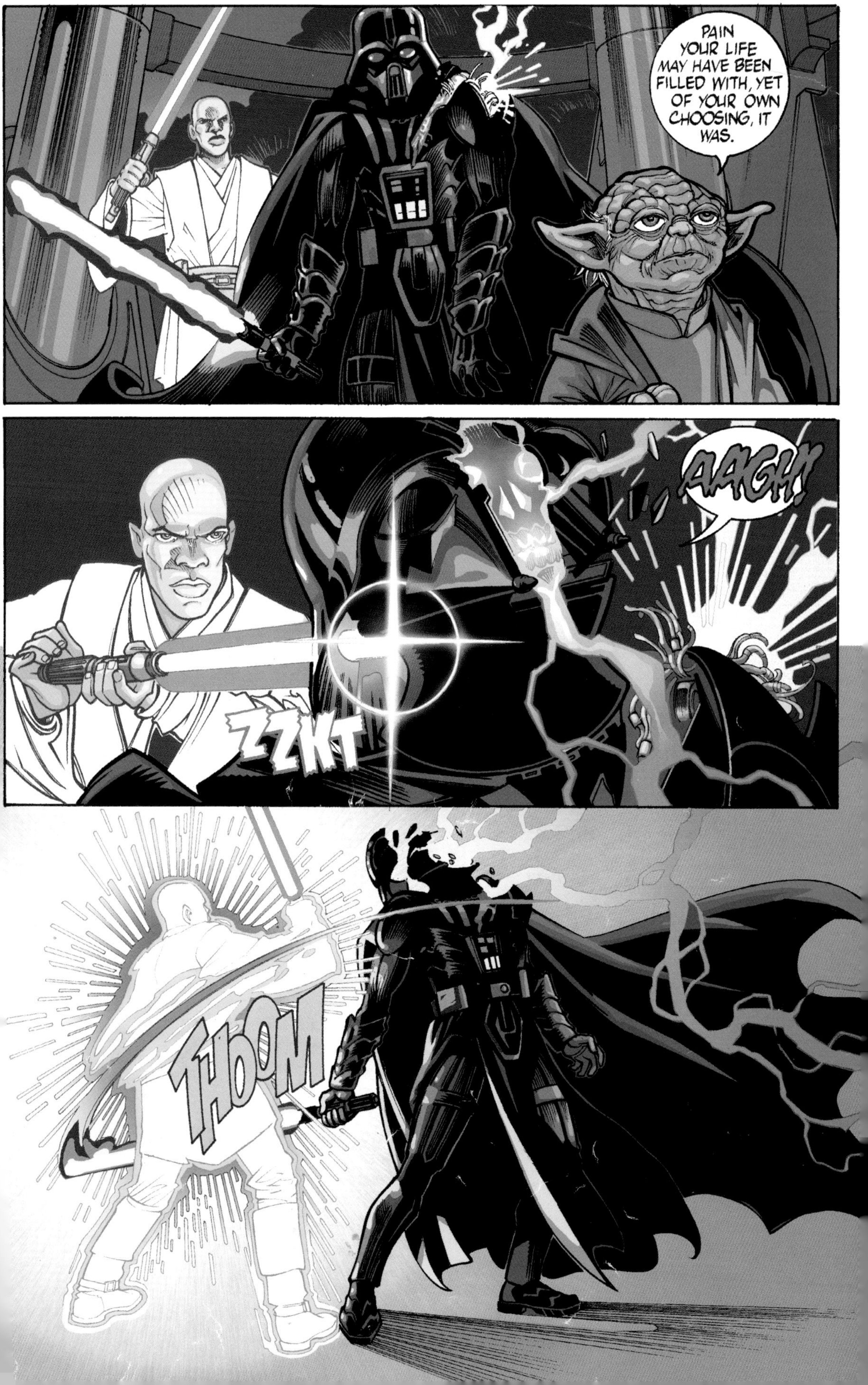
PAIN YOUR LIFE MAY HAVE BEEN FILLED WITH, YET OF YOUR OWN CHOOSING, IT WAS.
AAAGH!
ZZKT
THOOM

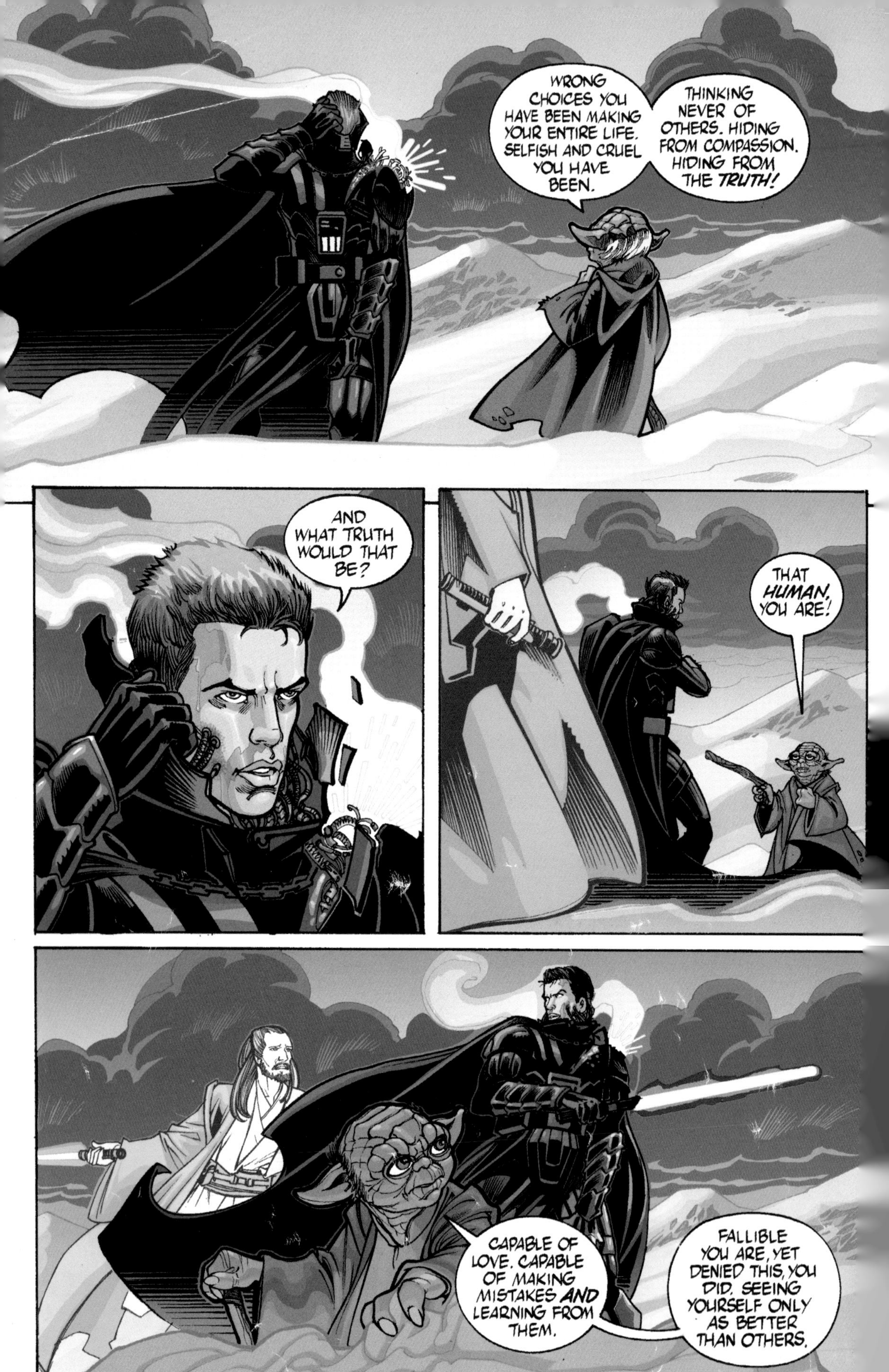
WRONG CHOICES YOU HAVE BEEN MAKING YOUR ENTIRE LIFE. SELFISH AND CRUEL YOU HAVE BEEN.
THINKING NEVER OF OTHERS. HIDING FROM COMPASSION. HIDING FROM THE *TRUTH!*
AND WHAT TRUTH WOULD THAT BE?
THAT *HUMAN*, YOU ARE!
CAPABLE OF LOVE. CAPABLE OF MAKING MISTAKES *AND* LEARNING FROM THEM.
FALLIBLE YOU ARE, YET DENIED THIS, YOU DID, SEEING YOURSELF ONLY AS BETTER THAN OTHERS.

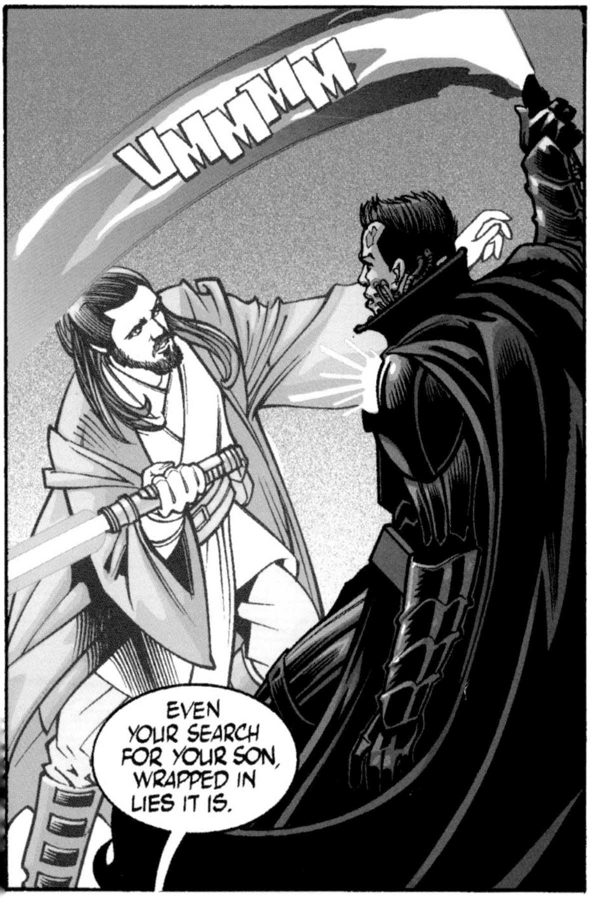
UMMMM
EVEN YOUR SEARCH FOR YOUR SON, WRAPPED IN LIES IT IS.

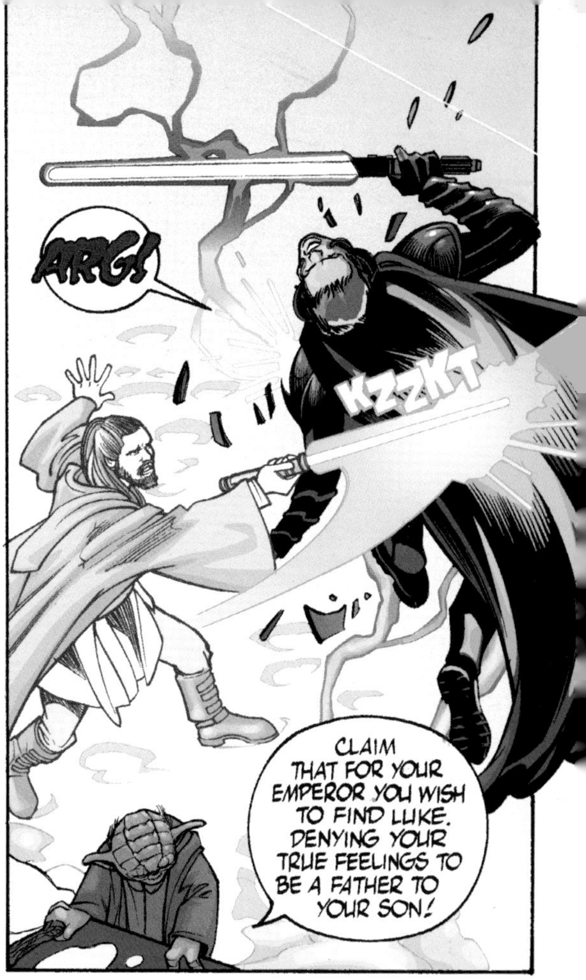
ARG!
KZZKT
CLAIM THAT FOR YOUR EMPEROR YOU WISH TO FIND LUKE. DENYING YOUR TRUE FEELINGS TO BE A FATHER TO YOUR SON!

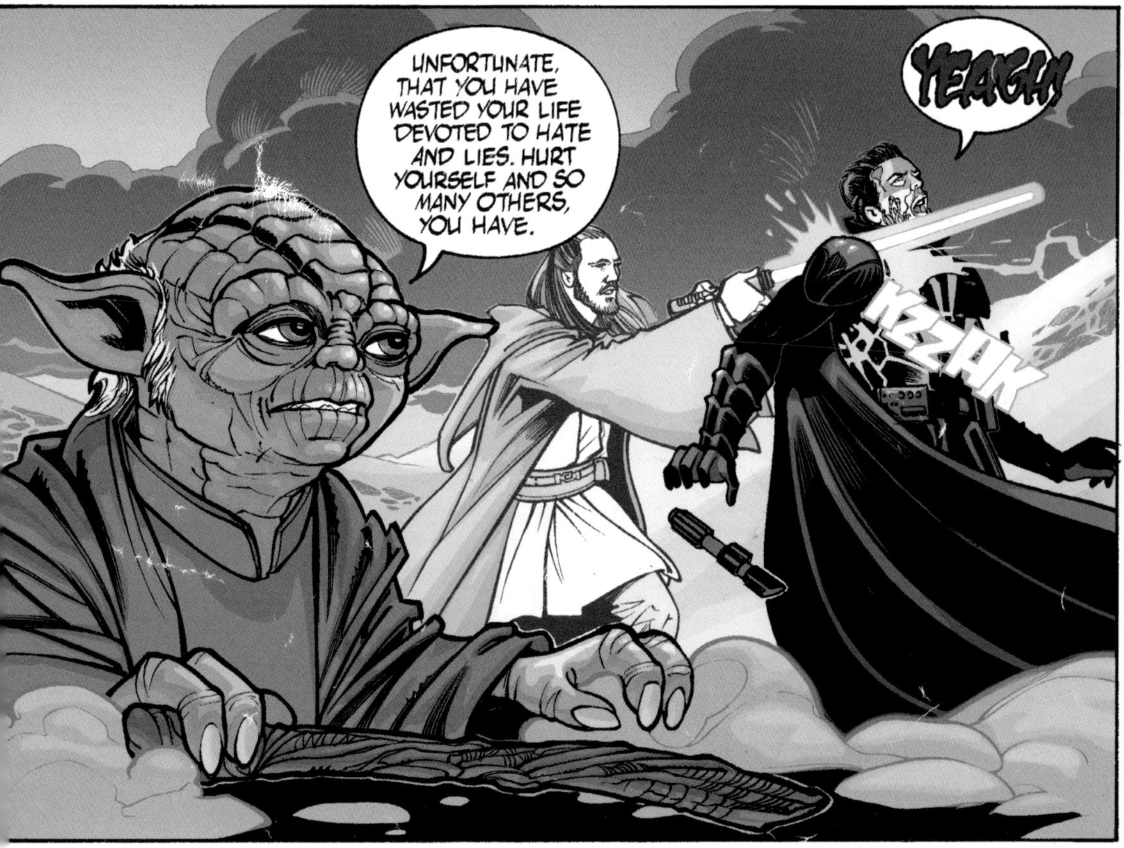
UNFORTUNATE, THAT YOU HAVE WASTED YOUR LIFE DEVOTED TO HATE AND LIES. HURT YOURSELF AND SO MANY OTHERS, YOU HAVE.
YEAGH!
KZZAK

ABOVE DAGOBAH...

OKAY, PAL. GET READY TO SET DOWN.

MRAWG GRAWWWPK WHRG!

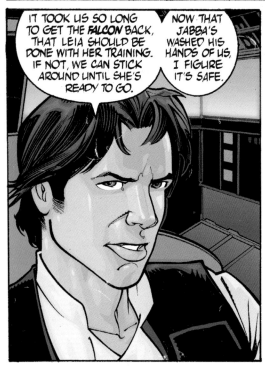

IT TOOK US SO LONG TO GET THE *FALCON* BACK, THAT LEIA SHOULD BE DONE WITH HER TRAINING. IF NOT, WE CAN STICK AROUND UNTIL SHE'S READY TO GO.

NOW THAT JABBA'S WASHED HIS HANDS OF US, I FIGURE IT'S SAFE.

BESIDES, I REALLY MISS HER.

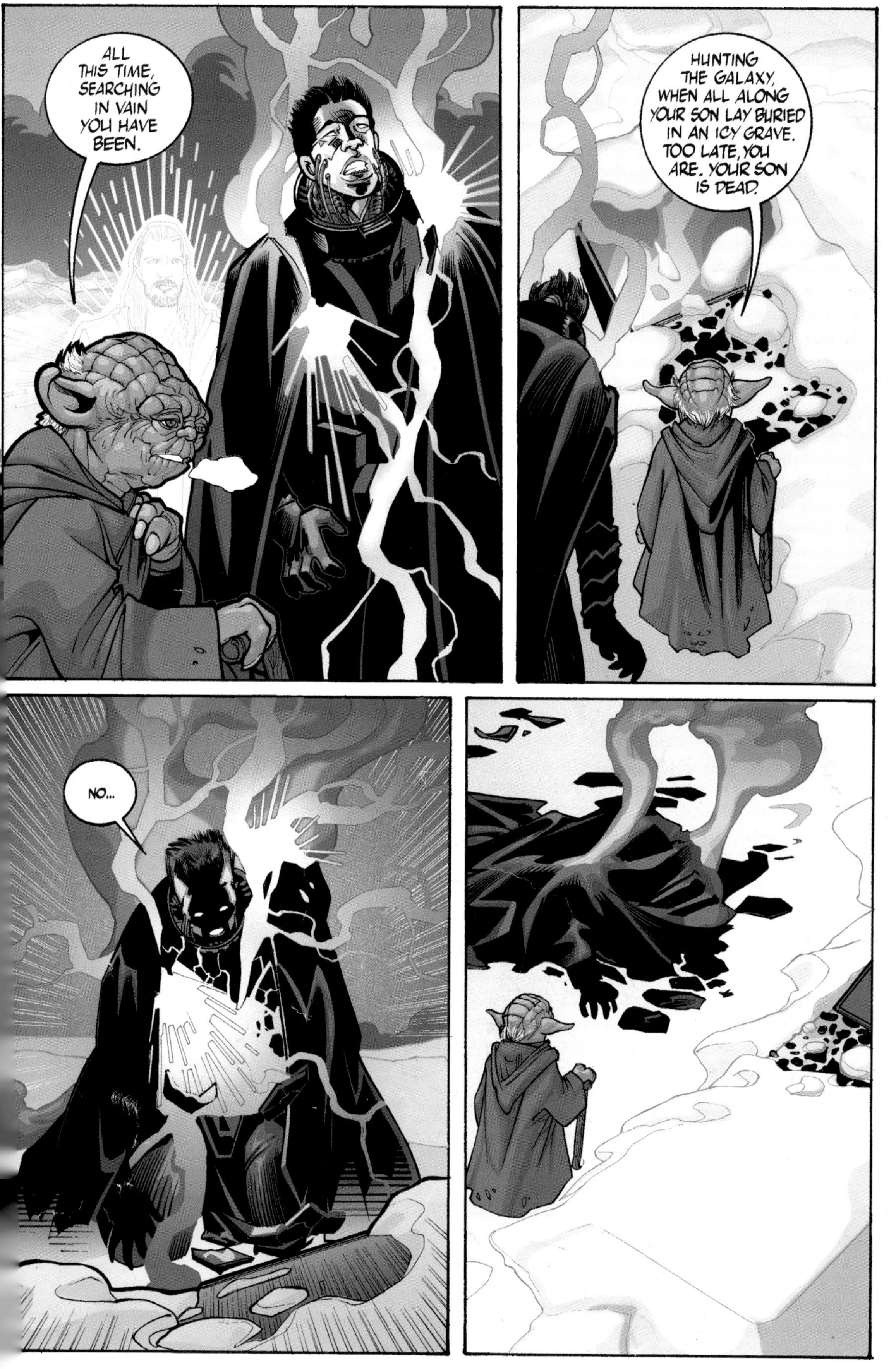
ALL THIS TIME, SEARCHING IN VAIN YOU HAVE BEEN.
HUNTING THE GALAXY, WHEN ALL ALONG YOUR SON LAY BURIED IN AN ICY GRAVE. TOO LATE, YOU ARE. YOUR SON IS DEAD.
NO...

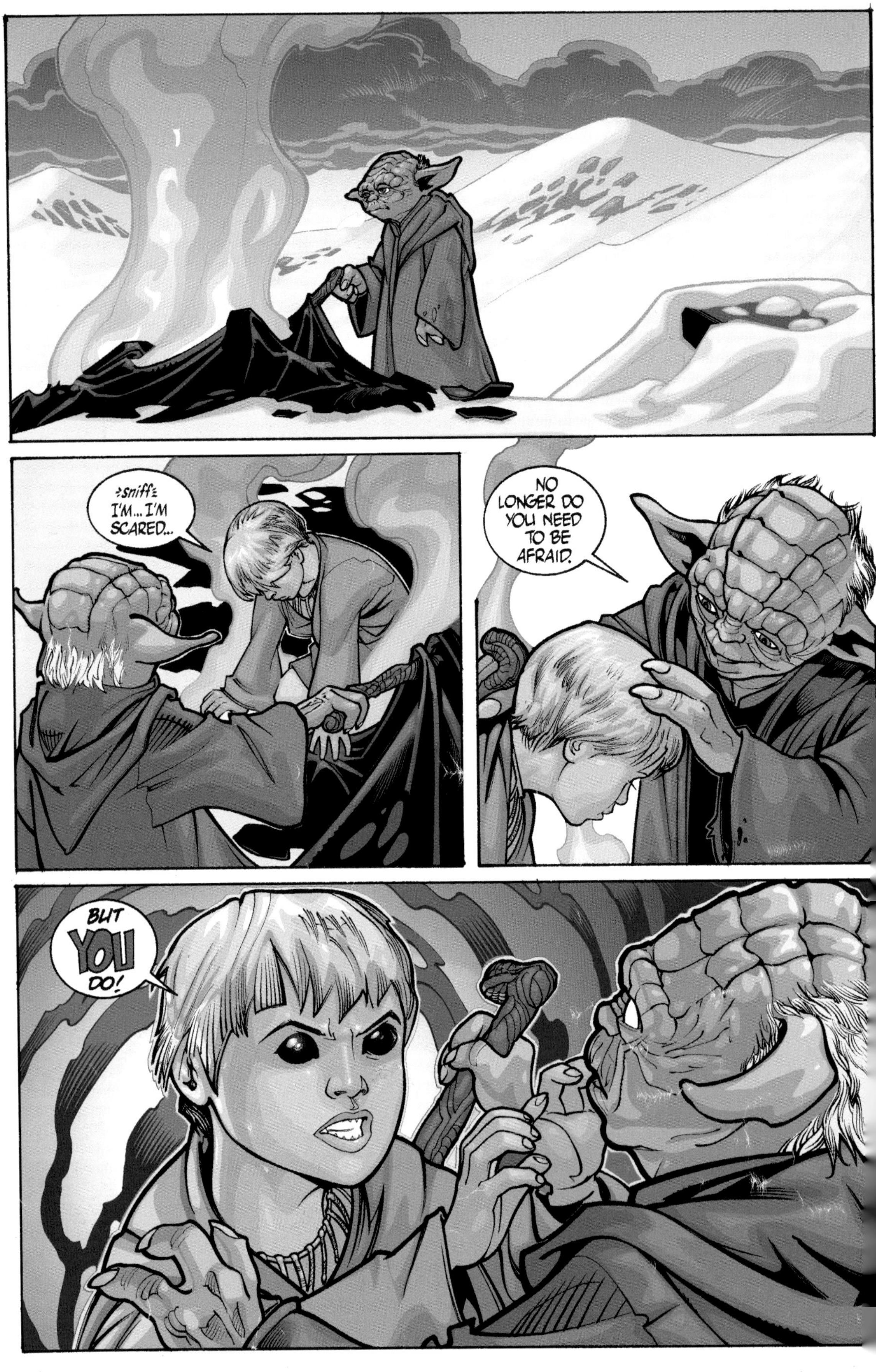

sniff
I'M... I'M SCARED...
NO LONGER DO YOU NEED TO BE AFRAID.
BUT YOU DO!

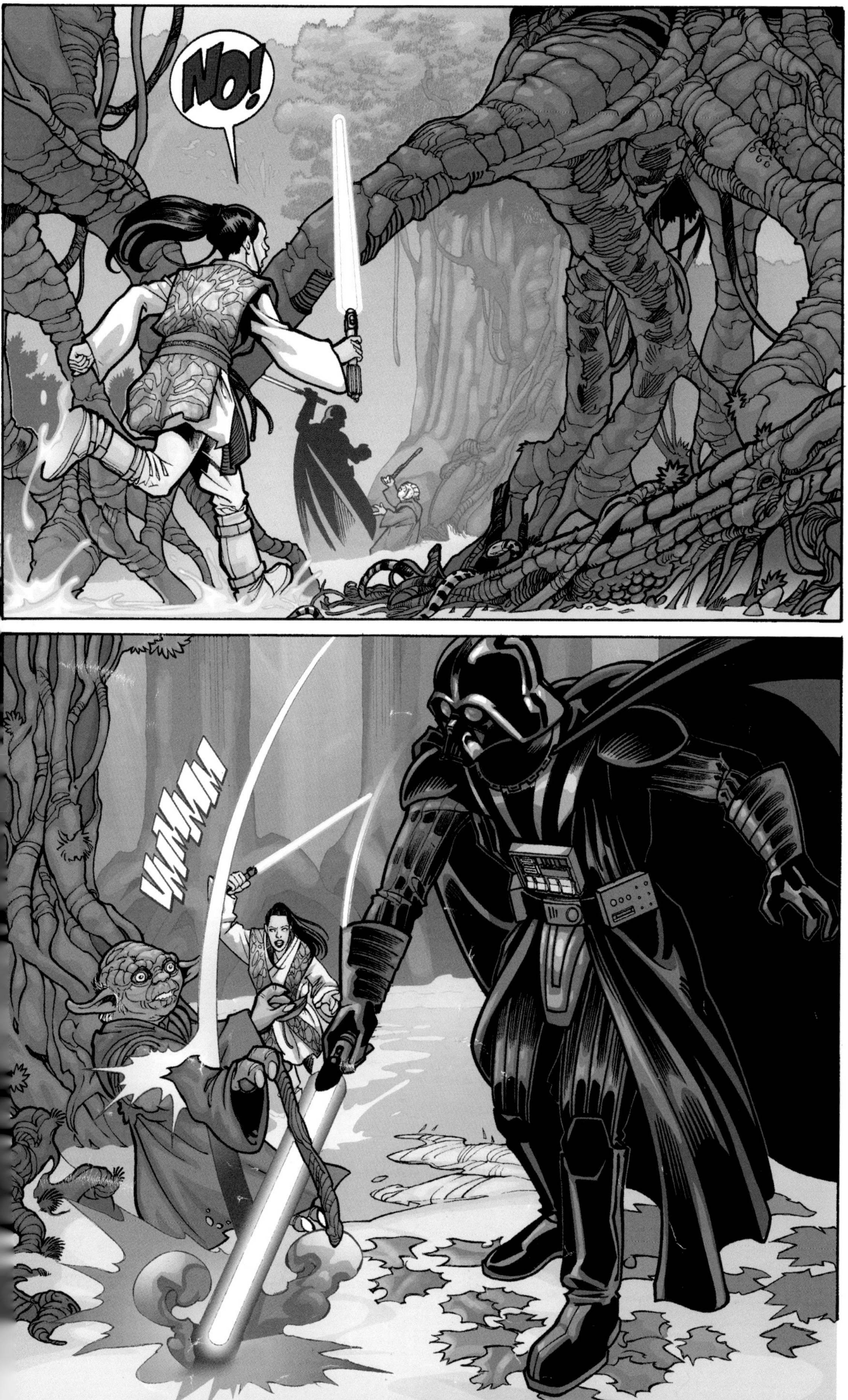
NO!

RAAGH!

ZZAK

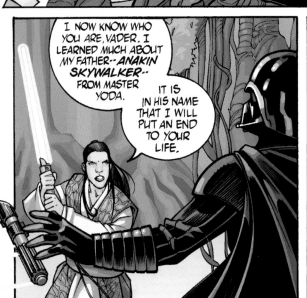

I NOW KNOW WHO YOU ARE, VADER. I LEARNED MUCH ABOUT MY FATHER--*ANAKIN SKYWALKER*--FROM MASTER YODA.

IT IS IN HIS NAME THAT I WILL PUT AN END TO YOUR LIFE.

I HAD GREAT PLANS FOR YOUR BROTHER.

THERE IS NO NEED FOR THEM TO DISAPPEAR ALONG WITH HIM.

YOU CAN JOIN ME.

I WILL NEVER JOIN YOU!

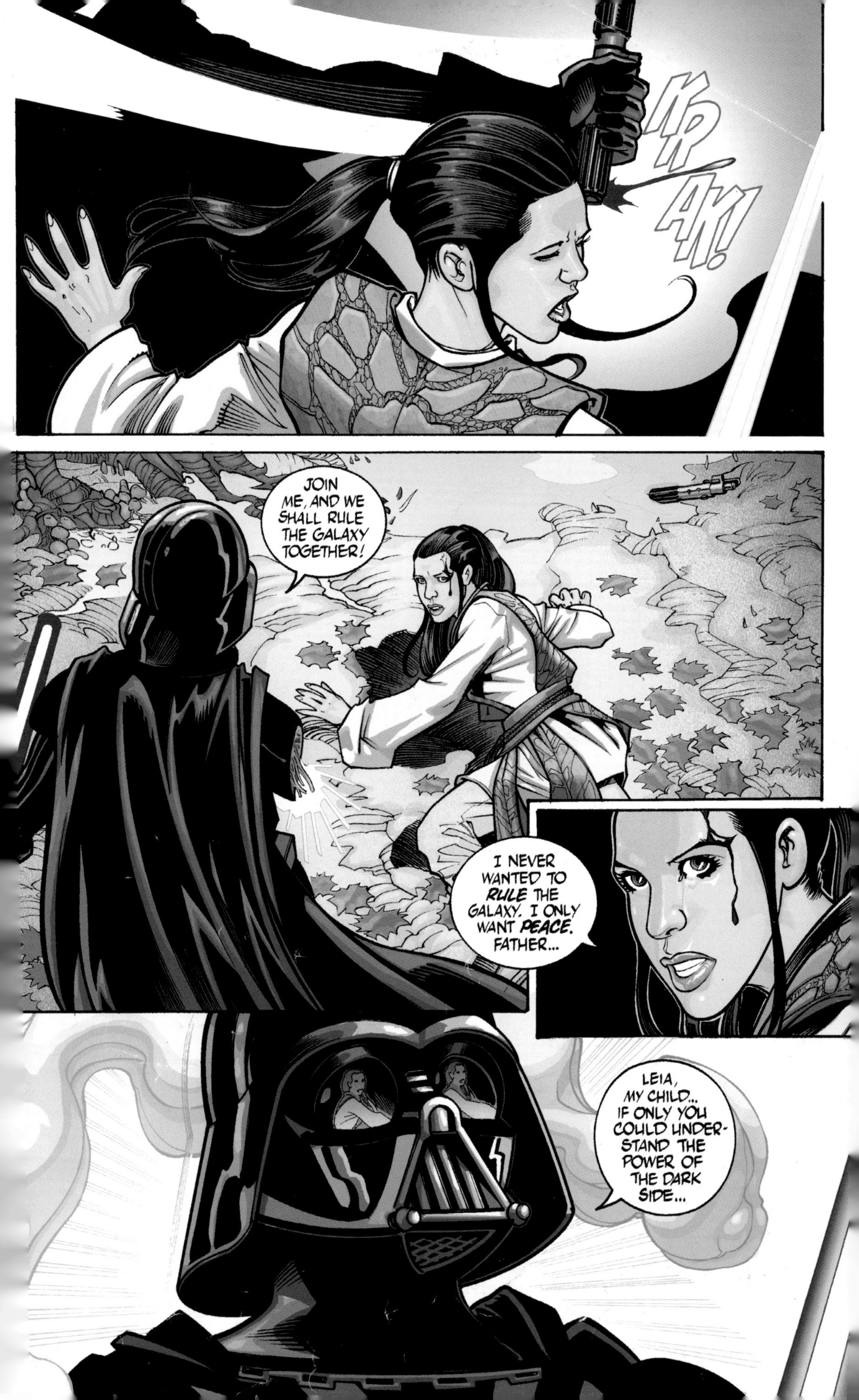
KRAAK!
JOIN ME, AND WE SHALL RULE THE GALAXY TOGETHER!
I NEVER WANTED TO RULE THE GALAXY. I ONLY WANT PEACE. FATHER...
LEIA, MY CHILD... IF ONLY YOU COULD UNDER-STAND THE POWER OF THE DARK SIDE...

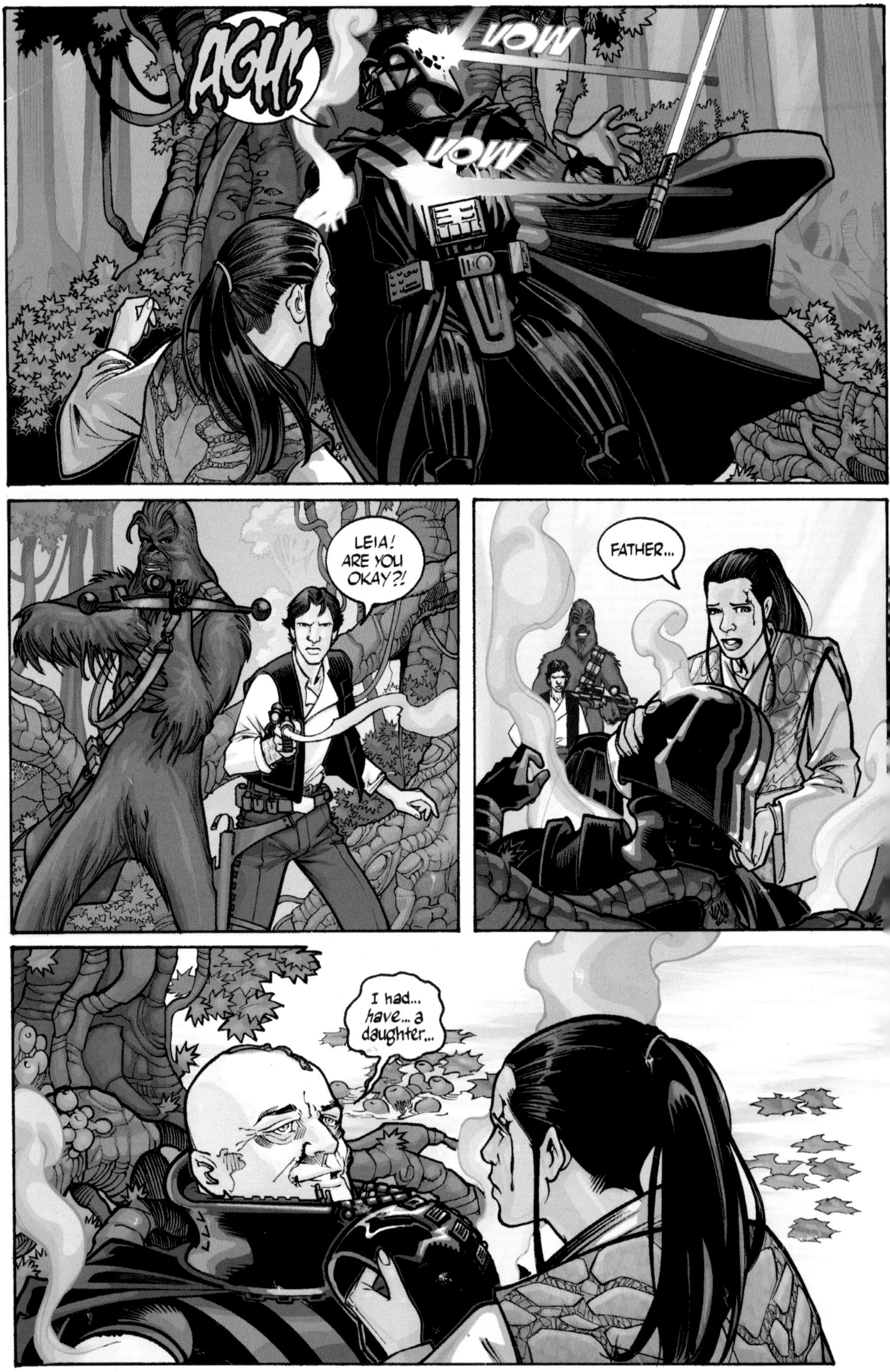
AGH!
VOW
VOW
LEIA! ARE YOU OKAY?!
FATHER...
I had... have... a daughter...

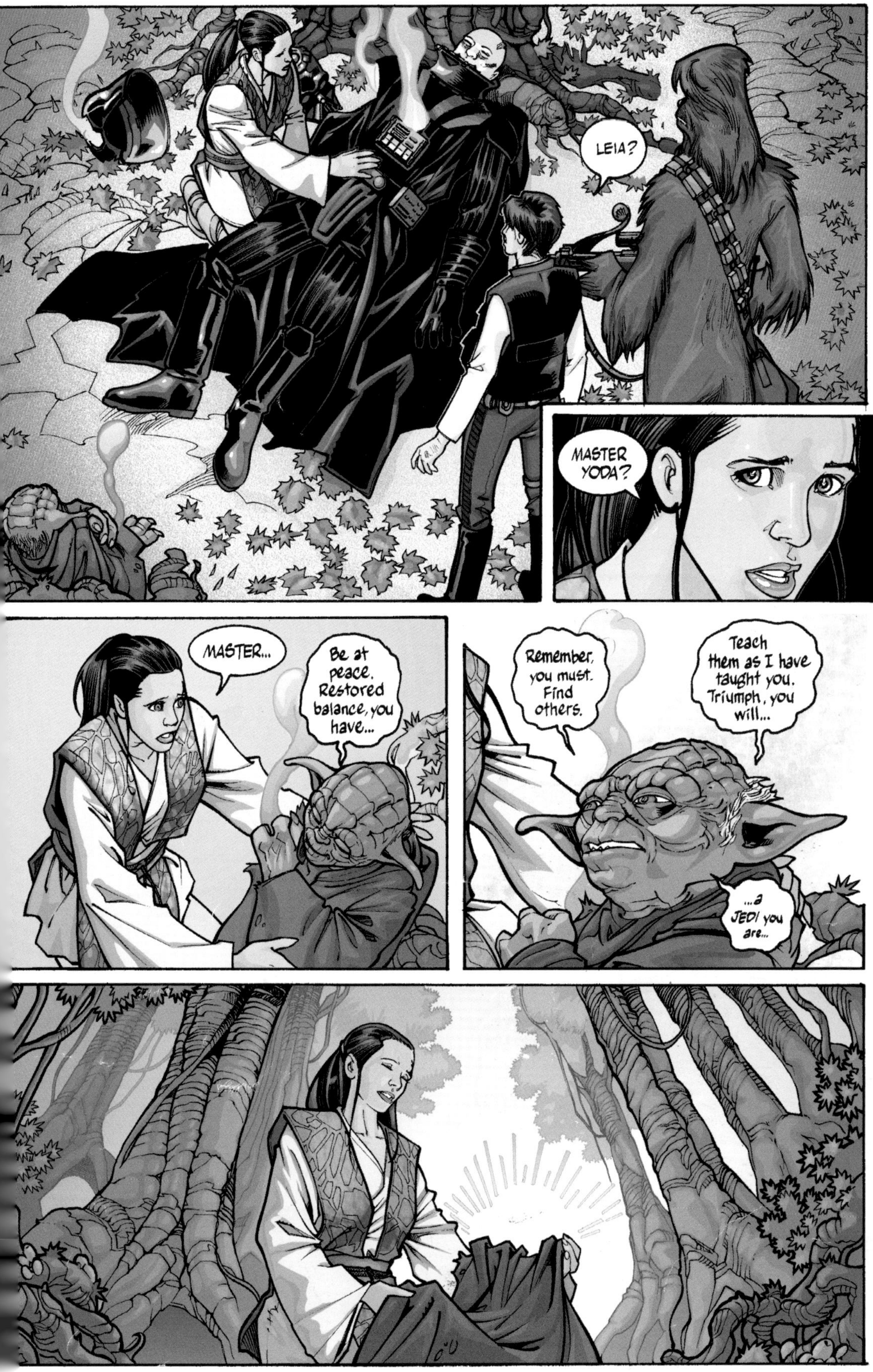
LEIA?
MASTER YODA?
MASTER...
Be at peace. Restored balance, you have...
Remember, you must. Find others.
Teach them as I have taught you. Triumph, you will...
...a JEDI you are...

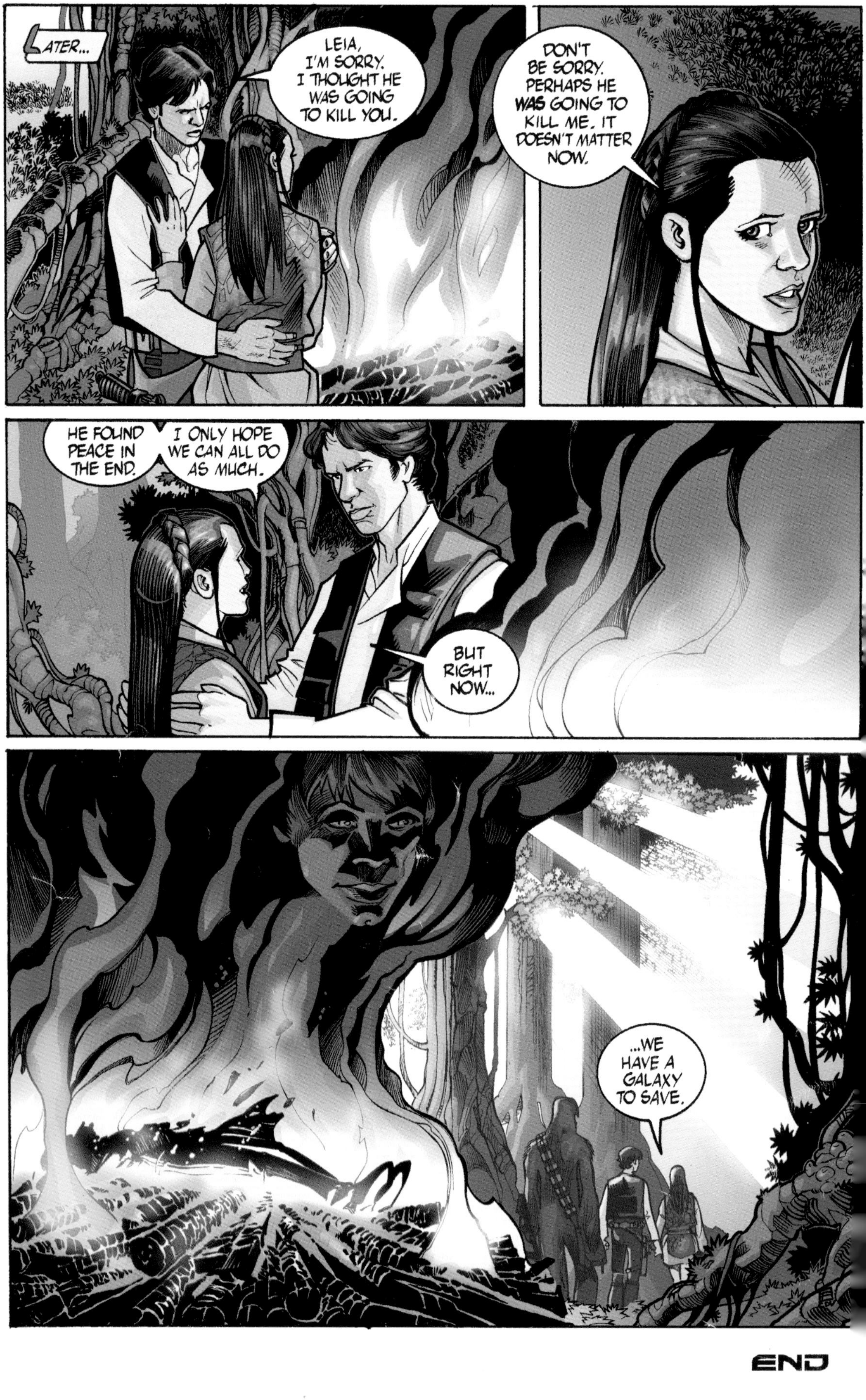
LATER...
LEIA, I'M SORRY. I THOUGHT HE WAS GOING TO KILL YOU.
DON'T BE SORRY. PERHAPS HE WAS GOING TO KILL ME. IT DOESN'T MATTER NOW.
HE FOUND PEACE IN THE END.
I ONLY HOPE WE CAN ALL DO AS MUCH.
BUT RIGHT NOW...
...WE HAVE A GALAXY TO SAVE.
END